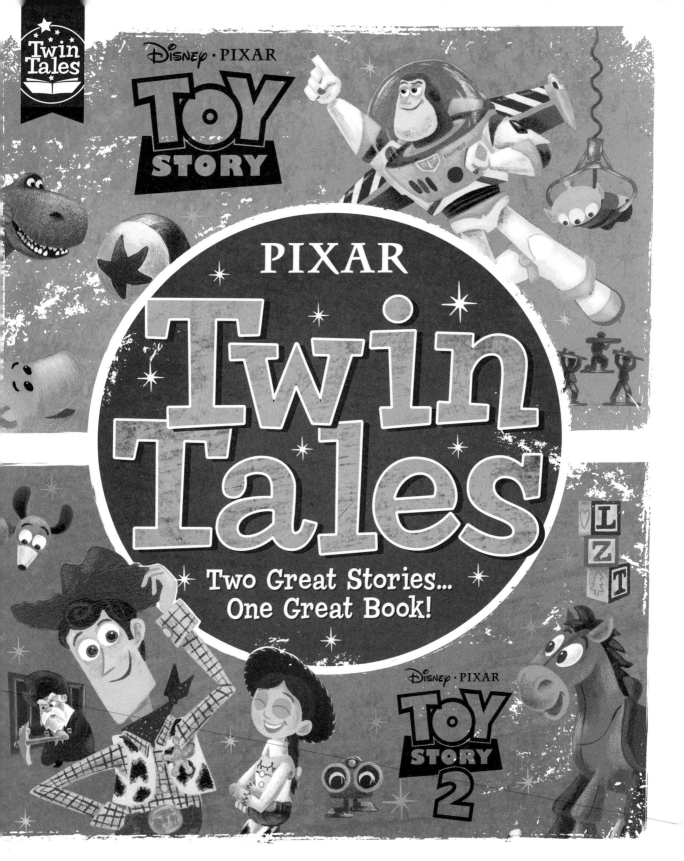

Twin Tales

DISNEY · PIXAR

TOY STORY

PIXAR

Twin Tales

Two Great Stories...
One Great Book!

DISNEY · PIXAR

TOY STORY 2

AUTUMN
PUBLISHING

AUTUMN
PUBLISHING

Published in 2021
First published in the UK by Autumn Publishing
An imprint of Igloo Books Ltd
Cottage Farm, NN6 0BJ, UK
Owned by Bonnier Books
Sveavägen 56, Stockholm, Sweden
www.igloobooks.com

1221 001
2 4 6 8 10 9 7 5 3 1
ISBN 978-1-80022-318-9

Printed and manufactured in China

This book belongs to:

....

Toy Story

Andy was a very lucky boy. He had lots of different toys.
But his favourite toy was a cowboy, named Woody.

Andy loved to play
with Woody.

But, there was something Andy didn't know about Woody and the other toys. When Andy wasn't around, the toys had a life of their own. They moved. They talked. They laughed. And they had adventures.

All the toys did. But only when no one was watching.

One year, Andy got a brand-new toy for his birthday –
a space ranger, named Buzz Lightyear!
Buzz had flashing lasers, gadgets and even wings.

Buzz thought he was a real
space ranger. He even thought
he could fly!

Woody tried to tell Buzz
that he was actually a toy.
But Buzz wouldn't listen.

Soon Buzz became Andy's new favourite toy. This made Woody very sad.

One day, Andy was going to Pizza Planet. His mum told him he could bring just one toy. Woody wanted to go! He tried to shove Buzz aside. But he accidentally pushed Buzz out of Andy's bedroom window instead. Whoops!

Woody got to go with Andy, but the other toys were very upset. They thought Woody had pushed Buzz out of the window on purpose.

Woody felt bad, until Buzz turned up in the car, too!

Buzz was angry with Woody. The two began to fight. When the car stopped at a petrol station, they tumbled out of the boot.

Oh, no! Andy and his mum drove off to Pizza Planet,
leaving Buzz and Woody behind. They had become lost toys!
And Andy's family was moving to a new home in just two days.

Then, Woody spotted a
Pizza Planet truck. Woody
told Buzz the truck was
a spaceship, and they
hopped on board.

Buzz insisted on riding in the front. Luckily a stack of pizza
boxes kept him hidden from the driver.

At Pizza Planet, Buzz climbed into a claw game filled with toy aliens. Buzz thought the game was a spaceship.

Woody tried to get Buzz out, but soon they were both trapped!

Oh no! Andy's mean neighbour, Sid, captured Buzz and Woody. Sid loved to torture toys. Woody and Buzz were in trouble! Sid took Buzz and Woody home with him.

Sid's room was full of mutant toys. He had created them by combining different toy parts in strange ways… and now he had evil plans for Buzz and Woody! They had to escape.

Buzz tried to fly out of Sid's house, but he fell. He finally realised that Woody was right – he wasn't a real space ranger. He was only a toy.

Sid strapped a rocket
to Buzz. He planned to
blow Buzz to pieces! Buzz
and Woody had to work
together if they were
going to escape.

But Buzz didn't want to escape. He felt sad because he wasn't
a real space ranger. Woody helped Buzz understand that Andy
loved him and that being a toy was very important.

And before they knew it, Buzz and Woody had become friends.

Woody came up with a plan to save Buzz. He asked Sid's toys to help. Just as Sid was about to blow Buzz up, Woody and the mutant toys came to life. Sid was terrified – he screamed and ran away.

Buzz and Woody were thrilled! So were Sid's toys. They knew that Sid would never torture them again.

Now Buzz and Woody were free to go back to Andy. But Andy's moving van was already pulling away from his house. They had to catch up to it!

Buzz and Woody ran and ran. Sid's mean dog, Scud, began to chase them!

Luckily, RC came out of the moving van to give Buzz and Woody a ride. They thought they were home free – until RC's batteries began to run down!

Then they remembered that Buzz still had Sid's rocket strapped to his back. Woody launched it.

WHOOSH! Buzz, Woody and RC flew through the air. RC landed safely in the back of the moving van. But Buzz and Woody kept going.

Buzz popped open his wings. The rocket flew into the air and exploded. Buzz and Woody were falling! But thanks to Buzz's wings, they were falling with style. Buzz held onto Woody and veered towards Andy's car.

Buzz and Woody glided through the car's sunroof and plopped down next to Andy – right where they belonged.

Toy Story 2

Do you like toys? Well Andy sure does. He has all different kinds of toys, and he loves to play with each and every one of them.

But Andy's favourite toys are a cowboy, named Woody...

... and a space ranger, named Buzz Lightyear.

One day, something terrible happened.

Woody was toynapped!

You see, Woody wasn't just a toy. He was a famous toy who once had his own TV show.

Along with Jessie the cowgirl, Bullseye the horse, and Stinky Pete the prospector, Woody starred in Woody's Roundup.

Because Woody and the other Roundup toys were so famous,
Al, a greedy toy shop owner, was going to sell them
to a museum, all the way across the world in Japan!

Jessie, Bullseye and Stinky Pete were
very excited. They had been in storage
for a long time.

But Woody didn't want to go to a silly museum!
He wanted to go back home to Andy!

That is, he did until Jessie
told him a story.
Just as Woody had Andy,
Jessie once had a little girl
who loved her.

They played together.

They laughed together.

They spent every day together – until the girl grew up and forgot all about Jessie.

Woody began to wonder if Andy would grow up and forget about him. Maybe the museum wouldn't be so bad after all…

Meanwhile, Buzz Lightyear had been busy planning a rescue mission.

Mr Potato Head,

Slinky Dog,

Hamm,

Buzz

and **Rex...**

...all set off together
to find Woody.

To get to Al's Toy Barn, the toys had to cross a busy street. Fortunately, they had a plan.

Success!

Inside the shop, Buzz and the others had to face another challenge – a new (and confused) Buzz Lightyear toy.

And little did they know that an evil toy named Emperor Zurg was hot on their trail!

But nothing would stop Buzz and his friends from finding Woody!

They quickly found Al in the office of the toy shop and
followed him to his flat – and there was Woody!

But there was one problem.

Woody had decided to go to the museum with the
other Roundup toys. He didn't want to end up forgotten
and in storage.

Buzz tried to convince Woody to go home to Andy, but the cowboy had made up his mind. So Buzz and the others left – without Woody.

It didn't take Woody long to realise that he had made a mistake. His true place was with Andy, not in a museum!

But Stinky Pete had a different plan. He was going to the museum, and no cowboy would stand in his way. He trapped Woody, Jessie and Bullseye in the flat. Then Al took them away.

Woody's friends had to rescue him, but first they had
to defeat Zurg!

Now they had to hurry – Al was on his way to the airport.
Next stop, Japan!

Buzz Lightyear to the rescue!
Buzz, Mr. Potato Head, Hamm,
Rex and Slinky borrowed a car
and raced to the airport.

They rescued Woody and Bullseye
and sent Stinky Pete packing!

Unfortunately,
poor Jessie got stuck
on the plane!

Would Woody and Buzz be able to save her?

Of course they would! Yee-haa!

Soon Woody, Buzz, Rex, Hamm, Mr. Potato Head and
Slinky were back in Andy's room – along with their new
friends, Jessie and Bullseye!

All the toys knew they couldn't stop Andy from growing up –
but they wouldn't miss it for the world!